# Gerd Conte's Dog Stories

# Gerd Conte's

# Dog Stories

# For Children

# CONTENTS

## VINCENZO, THE ITALIAN DOG

The dogs run from the beach to the restaurant when Luigi whistles. They know that lunch is over and the leftovers are waiting for them.

Luigi, the owner, but also the cook

in the little restaurant, never forgot his friends, the dogs. When the tourists left things like spaghetti, meat, clams or octopus on their plates, Luigi always saved them for the dogs.

On the beach, on a beautiful island off the coast of Italy, there were about 10 to 15 dogs, all colors and sizes. Some of them belonged to hotel owners, some to fruit-dealers on the main street, and others to the fishermen. A few of them were strays with no owner.

The dogs enjoyed the beach. They watched the fishermen mending their nets, listened to the voice of the sea, or laid under a shaded bench outside Luigi's restaurant. It often happened that there were more dogs on the beach than people, especially late in the summer when the tourist season was ending.

The dogs also enjoyed being with the tourists. Once in a while, people came to the beach who did not like dogs, so those kind of people usually moved to a fancy beach where no dogs were allowed.

Among the tourists was a fat lady in a pink bathing suit who always smelled of very strong perfume. She seemed to enjoy the dogs a great deal, because she was always surrounded by four or five of them. But she had taken an extra interest in a brown dog named Vincenzo, the smallest one on the beach.

He belonged to the pensione up the street, but spent most of the day on the beach.    Since the lady in the pink bathing suit had arrived, he had been with her all day long.  He knew that this friendship would not last long because tourists seldom stayed more than two weeks.  But Vincenzo was used to that, and after all, he still had his master.

The lady came to the beach at 8 o'clock every morning.  She rarely went for a swim, but spent most of the day in a beach chair, except for lunch, which she ate at Luigi's restaurant because nobody could make pasta like Luigi. She spent about an hour at the table, while Vincenzo was resting beside her. She usually gave him a portion of her own food. In addition to that, she gave him candy. Because the lady was not Italian, she spoke to Luigi in her own language, which was English.

When Luigi was not busy cooking, he was making little models of ships which he sold to the tourists. He had been a sailor once and had visited most of the famous seaports in the world.

One day the lady carried Vincenzo to her hotel room. She started to pack her suitcases, and every dog knows what that means. Then she gave Vincenzo a piece of candy which tasted very funny. Shortly after that, the dog felt sleepy. In fact, he had never felt so sleepy in his whole life. Soon he was fast asleep.

The lady lifted him up and put him in a basket. Soon she boarded a boat, then an airplane.

When Vincenzo woke up, he was in a strange room. The only thing he recognized was the lady. She smiled at him, gave him some milk, and pet him.

"Come, Vincenzo, let us go for a walk!" She put the dog on a leash, something Vincenzo had never seen before. They walked out on a big street, where the houses were three times as tall as the houses on the island that Vincenzo lived on.

In the days that followed, Vincenzo

was very homesick. He hated to be locked up in the apartment and could not stand the canned food the lady gave him. One day a friend of the lady visited her.

"Come and look at my dog," said the lady.

"How beautiful. What's his name?" asked the friend.

"Vincenzo."

"Ah, Italian!"

"Yes, I was in Italy last summer. I just love that country, so I thought I would give my dog an Italian name."

"Very interesting," said her friend.

But Vincenzo, who used to be a lively dog, was getting sadder every day. He was so homesick he hardly ate his food. The only thing that reminded him about home was the painting that hung on the wall. The lady had bought it as a souvenir in an art store on the island. There in the painting was the blue sea, the castle, the boats, and the beach. How well he knew all these things!

The painting brought tears to his eyes. One day he just kept on staring at the picture and crying until he finally fell asleep. He dreamed he was back on the island with all his friends. As Luigi was calling from the restaurant, they all ran and ate the leftovers. It was delicious meat in tomato sauce. And there was his master Salvatore, from the pensione among them.

When Vincenzo awoke, he was sad to realize it was only a dream. One morning the dog felt so weak he didn't get out of his little bed at all. The lady gave him some medicine that tasted just terrible. But nothing really mattered to Vincenzo anymore. All he wanted to do now was rest and sleep.

One morning the lady came down the front steps of her building. There the dog was lying quietly. She walked over and pet him, and spoke to him. But alas Vincenzo was dead.

The lady put the dog in her car and

drove out of the city. She found a forest, dug a hole in the ground, and buried him. Then she went back to the car, started it and drove off. She had only driven a few yards when she slowed down. She turned around and wanted to give Vincenzo a last farewell, but she could not see anything because her eyes were full of tears. She realized the terrible mistake she had made in thoughtlessly taking Vincenzo unlawfully from his true home.

## THE PUNISHMENT

Bikko lived in a land where the winter was long and cold. She was a big dog and strong enough to pull a sled.

When Lars, the boy in the family she

lived with, and Bikko drove through the village, people always stopped and talked to them. They told him how beautiful the dog was, and how kind Lars was to run all those errands for his mother. Lars was indeed a good boy. He was 8 years old and well known all over the neighborhood for his good marks in school and his kindness to the other pupils and his teachers.

But there was one boy in the village who didn't like Lars, and that was Folke.

He was several years older than Lars, and though he was his neighbor, they lived a couple of miles apart because the houses in that part of the country stood far apart.

When Folke heard the praise and attention that was often given to Lars, it was more than he could stand. For several months he had been trying to figure out a way to hurt Lars, and one day he came to the conclusion that the best way to hurt Lars would be to harm Bikko, because he knew that Lars was very fond of the dog.

That same day Folke's parents were going away to see some relatives in the next village. Only Folke's grandfather was left with him, but he was very old and hard of hearing, and spent most of his time in a rocking chair.

Folke saw this as a good chance to steal Bikko. He knew that every night at 6 o'clock the dog ran loose in the neighborhood. That night Folke was waiting outside the house for Bikko. The moon was shining, and the frozen lake looked like a carpet of crystal.

But Folke's thoughts were only on Bikko. He had a big bone with lots of meat on it ready. About 6:30 Bikko came running through the garden at Folke's house. When she heard Folke calling, she stopped for a moment, but when she smelled the big bone in Folke's hand, she came toward him. He walked into the kitchen and dropped it on the floor, and Bikko ran in after it. Then

Folke closed the door.

Folke kept Bikko in the guest room next to the kitchen. There were never any people there in the wintertime, and especially not his grandfather.

Lars could not understand why Bikko didn't come home that night. She always used to be home by 7 o'clock at the latest.

"Don't worry," said his mother. "Maybe she is out with her boyfriend!"

"Do dogs get married?" asked Ulla

who was only 4 years old.

"Yes, they do, but in a different way than people, and they have little baby dogs called puppies," said the mother.

"I hope Bikko comes back with lots of puppies," said Ulla as she put her dolls to bed.

There was no sign of Bikko the next day either. They looked for her all over the neighborhood, and asked everybody, but nobody had seen her. Lars was very unhappy. Where could she be? Could she be dead?  The thought made him cry.

Four days had gone by and Bikko was still locked up in the guest room. The heartless Folke seemed to enjoy every moment of it.

Then on the fifth day during the arithmetic class at school, the teacher was giving back the homework which he had corrected.  He richly praised some of the students, but when he came to Folke he said:  "And now, for you, Folke, your homework is all dirty and unclear.

Corners and margins on each page are torn; it is almost like a dog has gotten hold of it, but I know you don't have a dog. Therefore there will be no break for you today, and you have to stay for an extra hour to do it over again."

At first Folke didn't know what the teacher meant, but then he remembered that he had left his books in the guest room last night. Bikko must have played with them. He got red as a lobster in his face, but didn't say a word.

When Folke finally came home that night, he was not able to eat any of the food his grandfather had made. He just sat down on a chair staring at the floor. He sat like that for 10 minutes, then he walked over to the guest room and opened the door. He took one look at Bikko, opened the door to the garden and let her run out.

Folke walked out on the porch and stood there watching Bikko running toward her home. His eyes filled with tears as he realized how mean and heartless he had been. It was a cleansing experience for the good of his soul. He decided to offer Lars an apology and somehow make it up to him.

# A GROWN-UP AFRAID OF DOGS

There was a grown-up man who used to be afraid of doggies. His wife, who loved dogs, had asked him many times if she could get a puppy. But the man did not want to have a dog in the house.

He said: "Dogs bite and bark; they make holes in carpets; they chew on golf balls and beg at dinner tables. You have to take them for walks on rainy days, and when they come back, the first thing they do is shake themselves dry in the house. The furniture and carpet get dirty and wet. Who needs them?"

The wife tried to explain that if the dog was taught properly, such things would not happen. And if they do bite and bark, it is only because they are brought up that way, so that no burglars or strangers can break into the house.

But nothing could make the man change his mind.

Then one summer the couple went to visit the wife's family abroad, and in this home lived a dog. The day before they left, the man went to a store and bought some dog biscuits. The man hoped that food would calm the dog down, because the man had feared that this dog could be a very angry one.

So they sailed across the sea to a far-away land where people there spoke another language. The first to greet them when they arrived was the dog. His name was Rex, which means "King."

Rex came running down toward them and welcomed them by wagging his tail. He knew the wife, but he was just as friendly to the husband, even though the man was a stranger to him.

Rex looked at the man with his big

brown eyes, as if he were saying: "You don't have to be afraid of me, because I am good."

One of the first things the man did after he had arrived was to open his suitcase and take out the box of dog biscuits.

Rex thought they were delicious. He ate about ten of them, and it seemed the more he ate, the more he wanted. But then the man put the box away in the cupboard. Oh well, thought Rex, maybe

I'll get some more tomorrow.

The vacation days went by and Rex was certainly getting very fond of the man. If he went for a walk, the dog kept him company. If he went fishing, the same thing.

One afternoon the man wanted to go for a swim. His wife was busy helping her mother in the kitchen, so he decided to go alone. He had not walked far before he heard something behind him.

"I guess it's that dog again," he

thought to himself. "He is becoming a nuisance." And indeed there was Rex. The man looked at him and saw two big sad eyes. "Oh, well, come on then," he said. Rex quickly became very happy, and together they walked briskly down to the waterfront.

Rex had never seen anybody swim before. His master and his wife, who were the only people who lived on the farm, felt they were too old to go swimming. So when he saw the man jump in the water, he started to howl and cry. He thought the man was drowning.

But the man was having a wonderful time. The water felt cool and refreshing on this hot summer day. So he kept on swimming farther and farther away from the shore. Then all of a sudden he noticed something behind him. It was Rex! He grabbed the man's bathing suit and started to swim toward the shore. Then the man realized what a true friend Rex was. The dog had actually thought the man was drowning and wanted to save his life!

Nothing more was said about dogs, but that Christmas under the tree was a big brown box. There was no paper on it, just a label saying: "To my wife." When she opened it, she felt something moving inside, and just then — out crawled a tiny little puppy. It was the nicest gift anybody ever had given her!

## THE CURIOUS DOG

In a land far away from here, in a house close to a forest, lived a very tiny dog. In fact he was so tiny that his name was Tiny.

He was a good little doggie, but

always very curious. When somebody came to the house, he was the first one to run to the door to see who it was. If he heard a noise, he always had to find out what was going on.

Sometimes if he happened to hear something outside, he got so excited that he jumped up to the windowsill and then accidentally knocked down a flower vase or a small porcelain statue. The lady of the house then got mad at him and called him a naughty dog. Then Tiny felt so ashamed that he crawled under the couch with his tail between his legs.

His sense of shame never lasted long. Five minutes later he would hear something, and — oops! — out he would come. Tiny the curious dog never missed a thing. you see.

His bed was in the kitchen under the table. For a few nights now he had heard a funny noise. But he wasn't quite sure whether it was a cat, a bird or a baby. And there was no way of finding out because the doors were all closed and everybody was asleep.

After Tiny had heard the noise every night for about a week, he was dying of curiosity. What could it be? He never heard it during the day — only at night — and he just had to find out what the heck it was!

So one evening he decided that he would not go in at bedtime. The people in the house usually locked the doors about 9 o'clock because they got up very early in the morning.

That evening, Tiny found a place in the garden. There he laid under a tree, and when his master called him, he was quiet as a mouse. He heard the lady say to her husband, "I don't understand where Tiny could be." He couldn't help giggling a little.

"Don't worry," said the man, "he will be back when he gets hungry." Then they closed the door and got ready for bed.

The moon started to peek up behind the mountains and a few stars appeared in the clear sky. "What a beautiful night," thought Tiny. "Just perfect for an adventurer like myself!" He would simply lie there until he heard the noise again. Then he would follow it and satisfy his curiosity. "Oh, this is so exciting!" he said to himself.

After an hour of waiting, the same noise was heard again. "It has to be in the forest," Tiny said to himself. And he ran towards the big forest. Oh, it was very dark in there. But nothing could stop Tiny now...

Then suddenly, "Who are you?" said a deep voice. Tiny was startled and jumped back. There was a fox standing right in front of him. He had heard that foxes could be very dangerous, so poor Tiny ran as fast as he could.

"Ha, ha, he is afraid," he heard another animal in the forest say in a loud voice. It was a wolf speaking.

"What are you doing in our kingdom?" asked the wolf. The animals in the forest were not used to seeing little doggies, although on occasion they did see big hunting dogs zooming through the forest. But they had never seen a diminutive dog like Tiny before.

"Well, good evening, my friend, good evening," another animal said in a booming voice. Tiny felt the ground shaking beneath him. It was an enormous brown bear! Tiny got so afraid he decided he would go home. But where was home? He was completely lost, and he started to cry.

Then, all of a sudden, he heard that familiar noise again. He looked up and there, just above him in a tree, sat some kind of bird.

"I am wise; follow me!" said the bird, and off it flew. Tiny quickly ran in the same direction that the bird flew. Soon he recognized where he was. The bird landed on the top of the tree where

Tiny had laid and waited a few hours earlier.

"I am wisest of all the in whole animal kingdom," said the bird. "I am an owl, so always listen to me. Never go away from the house again." Then she flew back into the deep forest again.

Tiny walked up to the house and barked as loud as he could a few times. The man soon opened the door.

"Where have you been, you silly dog?" he asked. He let Tiny go out into the kitchen, and went back to bed.

Tiny took a few sips of milk and crawled into his bed under the kitchen table. The moon kept shining in through the kitchen window, and made funny shadows on the floor. But Tiny was too tired to even bother to get up and have a better look at what was going on. He was just so happy to be safely at home in his warm bed again.

## LISA, THE PEACEMAKER

L isa was a dachshund who lived on a farm in Norway. Dachshunds are not at all common in Norway and especially in the part of the country where Lisa lived. It seems that some relatives had brought her from Oslo, which is the busy capital city of this Scandinavian country, brought all the way to this farm which was high up in the mountains.

Lisa was a lovely little dog. As long as she had enough to eat and plenty of love, she was very happy. And she had plenty of both. Everybody was very fond of the sweet little dog, and the family always made sure she got the best possible care and plenty of love.

One day Martha, the woman on the farm, was going down to the village to do a few errands, and she decided to bring Lisa with her.

Lisa had never been in the village before. In fact, she had never been away from the farm at all since she arrived on a summer day two years earlier.

The ride from the farm to the village took a half-hour by bus, and Lisa sat on Martha's lap the whole time. Everybody in the bus kept on looking at this rather unusual passenger; for it wasn't very often that riders saw dogs on buses.

A few boys were sitting in the back seat, making jokes about Lisa. One said: "Are we in a cattle-carriage?"

When the bus stopped in the village, Martha and Lisa got off. They walked around a bit, went into a few stores, and then to some sort of business office, and finally Martha stopped for a visit at a friend's house.

The friend greeted her and asked

her to come in. Martha left Lisa outside, thinking it would be nice for the dog to run around freely for a while.

Some children who were playing next door soon noticed Lisa. They had never seen a dachshund before.

"Look at the funny dog with such short legs," said one.

"It's like a walking sausage!" said another youngster.

"Yes, let's get some mustard and rolls and have him for lunch," laughed the third one.

Within a few minutes, Lisa was surrounded by children from all over the neighborhood. There were perhaps a dozen kids looking at Lisa and all were making funny jokes about her. Poor Lisa felt so bad; she wished she had never come to the village. She was longing for the farm, where everybody knew her, and nobody made fun of her.

Among the children who were very intently observing little Lisa was a 10-

year-old girl by the name of Karin. She

was supposed to look after her little baby

sister, who was only a year and a half

old. But in all the excitement over Lisa,

she had forgotten about her sister!

But dogs have good ears, and when

Lisa heard the baby cry, she ran down the

road to see what it was. There was the

little baby girl lying in the middle of the

road. The child had a few streaks and

blemishes on her face, but most of it was

just dirt. Lisa dragged the baby to the

side of the road. Then she licked the baby's face clean.

By now, all the children were gathered at the rescue spot and everybody was very quiet. Karin felt so ashamed. Not only had she forgotten to look after her little sister, but she had made fun of the dog — this dog that was so ready to help in time of danger!

All of a sudden, somebody was calling out Lisa's name. It was Martha. "Time to go home!" When the bus pulled out from the bus station in the village with Martha and Lisa looking out the window of the bus, there were all twelve local kids were standing on the platform, waving and shouting: "Lisa, come back soon!"

## A COLLIE FINDS A NEW HOME

O n a cold day in late autumn, a long-haired collie named Juno was sitting on a door step looking up at gray clouds that covered the sky.

A few snowflakes began to fall, and

it made Juno very sad. The season of cold weather, ice and snow on the roads, and nasty winds was just around the corner, and she knew that she was going to suffer a great deal.

For some doggies, the winter season is hardly anything to worry about. They have lots of fun playing with the children in the snow, and if it gets too cold, they just go inside and lie in front of the fire to take the chill out of their bones.

But for Juno it was different. There

were no children to play with in the house where she lived — and the married couple didn't really care too much about her anyway. A few times Juno had even heard the man say to his wife: "Why don't you get rid of that dog?"

Sometimes they went away for several days at a time, and all Juno had to eat was the scraps of food she picked out of other people's garbage cans, or what the neighbors gave her out of kindness.

Often when it was cold, Juno sat

outside, hoping that the master or else his wife would let her in the house. A few times the door was left open and Juno had snuck inside, but as soon as the owners discovered her, they started to yell at her, saying she made big marks on the carpet.

And then they would open the door and tell her to go outside again. At night Juno was allowed to sleep in the hall, but that was only if the people were home. If they went away for a few days, Juno had to stay outdoors, no matter how cold it got.

In the summertime Juno liked very much being outside. It was wonderful to lay in the garden and listen to the birds, watch them fly, or even chase a cat or a squirrel once in a while. And somehow there was always more to eat during the summer months.

It would be a long time before summer came again. That's why Juno was sad today, sitting on the door step watching the snow fall.

"Well, it's no good just sitting here and sulking. I'll go for a walk. At least it will keep me warm," Juno said to herself.

The dog walked towards the forest. The snow was falling heavily now, and the wind was getting stronger.

To her joy and surprise, the forest was a shelter for Juno. The ground was almost dry, and she could hardly feel the wind blowing. She eagerly walked along a narrow path and soon reached the end of the forest.

Once outside the forest again there was a lot more snow on the ground, and the wind blew so hard that Juno had the feeling it would blow her over. It was getting darker now, and there was so much snow in Juno's eyes, she could hardly see.

Then suddenly she saw a dark wall in front of her. Could it be a house?

"Yes, that's what it is! I can find

shelter there," Juno told herself as she quickly trotted towards the house.

Inside the house, a family of four were gathered around the dinner table. It was Mr. and Mrs. Wood, their son Paul, age 6, and his 2-year-old sister Sonja.

"It is going to be a very stormy night," said Mr. Wood.

"Yes, a night to be thankful for a house to live in! And not everybody has a house, you know," replied Mrs. Wood.

"Why doesn't everybody have a

house?" asked Paul.

"Wait!" said his father. "I thought I heard something."

"It's probably just the wind," said Mrs. Wood.

But her husband got up anyway and walked over to the door. He opened it and saw Juno sitting on the icy steps, shivering in the cold.

"A dog!" he cried out.

"Let it come into the house!" yelled Sonja from the dining-room table.

In walked Juno looking like a living snowman, or rather a living snowdog. She shivered as pieces of snow flew off her body. Soon the whole family became very excited over helping the poor dog. One came with a towel to wipe her dry, one with a bowl of warm milk, one with food, and little Sonja wanted to give the dog her own pillow.

Juno ate like she had never seen food before. Soon she was sound asleep in front of the fire.

That night Paul was lying in his bed saying a prayer. Christmas was only two weeks away. It didn't matter if he didn't get the skis, the electric trains, or any of the other things he had asked for in his letter to Santa Claus.

"If only I can keep the dog," he prayed. He had always wanted a dog, and this one seemed so nice and kind — but also very sad and in need of love. Maybe Juno was sad because she didn't have a house to live in? After all, his mother had told Paul that not everyone had a house of their own to be happy, and he wanted very much to make this nice dog so happy.

Christmas finally came, and nobody had asked about Juno, or came to the house to claim her. So Paul got his Christmas wish to keep Juno, and she became a member of the Wood family. They named her "Snowdog," since they never knew her real name. The dog soon got used to her new name and would come running whenever she heard it.

Now each and every winter season Snowdog watches for the first snowflakes to fall. But it never makes her sad like it used to. In fact, it makes her very happy now. She knows that if it hadn't been for the snow, she probably never would have found the Wood family — a family that changed her life from that of a very sad dog into the happiest and best loved dog in the world.

## PRINCE AND THE PRINCESS

Prince was the smartest dog in the neighborhood. He could fetch his master's slippers, he could get the newspaper, and he could even shake people's hands when they came to the house. Yes, this was a dog that could do many unusual things.

His master had taught him all these things when he was a puppy. And if Prince forgot any of them — well, there was only one thing to do, and that would be to learn whatever he had forgotten all over again!

Now because the dog was so clever, he became everybody's pet. People were fascinated by the things he could do, and for a reward they often brought him candy, cookies and toys.

Prince had a good life. He lived in a big house with his master, the master's wife, and their daughter Anne.

"Yes, it's nice to be alive," thought Prince, as he rolled lazily in the sun. The delicious smell of cooking was coming from the kitchen, and he could hear chairs being moved and people talking. Today was Anne's birthday, and she was going to have a party.

"I'm going to be the center of

attention!" Prince thought proudly, if not a little mistakenly.

In a little while he heard children talking and laughing, and then Anne came to the door and called out, "Prince, come. We are going to start the party!"

Prince ran up to the house and extended his paw to shake each child's hand in a friendly way.

"Isn't it wonderful what he can do," somebody said.

"Yes, and he's so clever!" another

one said.

Prince wagged his tail happily. There were cakes and other goodies on the table, but Anne could hardly wait until the meal was over, because that's when she would get to open her presents. She looked over at the other table and saw a whole pile of very exciting and colorfully-wrapped boxes.

After the meal, Prince was watching Anne while she opened her gifts. There were dolls, dresses, toys, books, clothes and other things. Then while she opened a big box, everybody seemed to be extra excited. What could this be? Prince inched closer, and then he saw a tiny black and white head peeking out. It was a cat!

"My happiness is over," thought Prince as he walked away and crawled under the couch. But nobody had even noticed that. They were too busy playing with the new cat. Anne even named her Princess, and that seemed to please

Prince a little at least as he perked up to take it all in…

Prince carefully watched Princess for the next three or four days. When nobody was around, he chased her as much as he could, but Princess was always the quickest one. She jumped up on the table without any difficulty, and she had no trouble getting to the top of the bookshelf, something Prince would never ever try to do.

One day Anne walked into the

living room and found Princess sitting on top of the china cabinet, looking with scared eyes at a barking Prince. Anne got angry at Prince and told him never to do it again. But nothing seemed to stop Prince's anger toward Princess. One day the dog chased the cat so much that the cat disappeared. The people looked all over for her, but there was no sign of her. Anne was so upset she would not touch her supper that evening.

"Princess will come back," said her

mother trying to comfort the girl.

"No, she will not. Prince chased her away. It's all his fault," said Anne. She went to her bedroom and cried for a long time.

Two days went by and there was still no sign of Princess. The first thing Anne asked about when she came from school was, "Has anyone seen the cat?" But the answer was always the same.

Prince himself was still going around shaking people's hands and getting the slippers for his master, but somehow it wasn't fun for him any more, and — worse yet — Anne didn't play with him like she used to do, either.

The dog felt so bad that one night he wasn't able to sleep. It was all his fault, he now thought. He had made the cat disappear; he had made Anne and her parents unhappy; and, on top of all that, he had made himself very unhappy, too.

His master and his wife had been so good to him, and Anne had been his best friend for a good many years. When he thought about it, had Princess done him any harm? No, she had not. It was not her fault that she had been brought into this house as a birthday gift for Anne.

That night Prince didn't sleep even for five minutes, but when the morning came he made up his mind about what to do. *He was going to find Princess!*

As soon as the door opened, Prince ran out. He was running and sniffing around the whole morning. He looked in the forest, on the hill behind the rocks, and had almost given up hope when he spotted a broad cluster of wild raspberry bushes. There, hidden in the bushes, what could that be?

Prince walked closer and there was a lonely Princess, thin and with dull, dry, roughed-up fur. Drops of blood were dripping from one of her eyes. When she saw Prince, she became so afraid that she tried to run away, but she was too weak to get very far. She fell down on her side and laid there trembling with closed eyes.

"I have to get help immediately," thought Prince. So with a heart full of sadness, he ran as fast as he could back home.

The people were having lunch when Prince came running into the house. He stopped in the middle of the kitchen floor and started to bark.

"What's the matter with this dog — is he getting violent?" asked Anne's father.

"Go with him," said his wife. "He wants to show you something."

The man dutifully followed Prince and together they soon found Princess, who was still lying in the same place. The man carried her carefully home in his arms while Prince walked faithfully behind him.

For a few days it seemed as if Princess was not going to make it, even though she had the best possible care. They kept Prince completely away from the ailing kitten.

But one day when Princess started to drink milk and eat a little food, there was lots of new-found joy in the house. Gradually she recovered and became a spry, beautiful and healthy young cat again.

One day Prince walked into the living room where Princess was stretched out and relaxing. When he saw the cat he started to wag his tail, then walked towards her and even laid down next to her. The cat was a bit wary but remained where she was.

Soon the whole family saw that Princess didn't run away, but seemed rather to enjoy Prince's warm, friendly company. Everyone was amazed! But Princess had known, ever since that morning under the wild raspberry bushes when rescued by Prince, that the dog was not angry at her any more, and that his loving concern for her was very great indeed.

# THE POODLE IN A PENTHOUSE

In a penthouse on Park Avenue in New York City lived a poodle named Peter. The owner was a lonely lady who had no husband, no children, no relatives, and very few close friends, either. But she was rich and spent a lot of money on Peter. He had a mink coat, a jewel-studded collar, a raincoat, boots and other nice things. Every month he got a shampoo and haircut at the poodle shop. They even perfumed him and brushed his fluffy white hair!

When the lady took Peter for a walk in Central Park, people would stop to look at him. Everybody thought he was a beautiful dog. And Peter was not only beautiful — he was a good dog, too.

Back when he was a puppy, his mama had told him:

"You must always be nice to your master. Do only what she wants you to do. Follow her, be faithful, wait for her, watch over her and love her with all your heart. Never forget that."

The lady was Peter's master, and he had been with her since he was 6 months old. He was now almost 3 years of age, and during this growing-up period he had always tried to do what his mama had told him.

One afternoon Peter was alone in the big living room. The lady was resting upstairs, the butler had gone on an errand, and the maid had the day off. Usually when Peter was alone, he went to sleep because there was nothing else to do. But this afternoon was different and he felt like doing something.

Outside the sun was shining, the air was crisp and cool. It was a beautiful October day and Peter started to look around the room. A couch, chairs, a table, paintings, it was all so familiar — and boring. On the coffee table was a picture book of dogs that the lady had been reading. Peter could easily reach it, so he took it in his mouth, lowered it to the floor, and started to slowly and methodically flip through the pages with his right paw.

There were pictures of big and little doggies, fat ones, thin ones, long ones and short ones. Then he soon came to a picture and stopped: it was a poodle exactly like himself. But this poodle was outside in a field running with a stick in its mouth while playing with a boy. The boy was smiling broadly and the dog seemed so happy, too.

Then Peter became very sad. He wished he had someone to play with also, or at least a place where he could run around without being on a leash. He started to walk around the room and stopped in front of the big mirror in the hallway.

"I don't even look like a normal dog," he said to himself. But as he was looking in the mirror he noticed something. Was it a tree? He turned around. No, it was only a plant. "Hey," he thought, "that could be something to play with!"

He grabbed the plant in his mouth and started to run around the room. The beautiful carpet was soon covered with dirt from the flower pot and leaves torn from the plant were scattered all over the room.  Peter was yelping and barking — he never had so much fun in his life!

Then the door opened, and in came the butler, back from his errand.

"I don't believe it!" he cried, and ran upstairs yelling loudly.  "Madam, madam!  The dog has gone crazy!"

The lady came running down, and shortly after she was on the phone, excitedly telling the dog doctor — known as a veterinarian — what she thought happened. She was sure the dog was very sick, but the doctor told her not to worry, and that it sounded to him like the dog just wanted to have fun. The lady listened patiently to the vet's advice on what to do, thanked him, and hung up the phone.

Since that day the lady decided to take Peter for a drive every Sunday. She takes him to the country where he can run around without a leash, and every time he is there, Peter thinks of the

poodle in the picture book.  Now he is

just as happy as him.

# THE STORY OF JENNY

# AND SHADOW

Jenny, a Belgian shepherd, and Shadow, a French poodle, lived in a big house just inside the border of New York City. They were happy dogs — both of them females — and they had a good life because the people in the family were dog lovers.

Jenny was 3 years old, and full of life and curiosity. Shadow was 7, quiet and full of wisdom. She was named Shadow because she had always followed her master or his wife, even as a small puppy.

Summer had come, and the family had gone on vacation. Only the maid and the cook remained at home to look after the two dogs.

Late in the afternoon on a hot day, the two dogs were laying in the garden. The days were always longer when the people were away, and even though the cook took them for a walk every day, they still missed the daily afternoon drive in the car which the wife usually gave them.

The cook claimed she could drive, and a few times she took Jenny and Shadow for a ride. But the dogs thought she was a terrible driver, and by the time they came back to the house, they were both a nervous wreck.

One day the cook bumped the car into the fence just outside the kitchen window. She was never able to put the car into the garage. So unless the dogs could go for a drive with the husband or the wife behind the wheel, they preferred not going for a drive at all.

"Well, this is better than being in a kennel," said Jenny.

"That's for sure," said Shadow. She

never forgot that year she spent in a kennel. "And after all, the maid and the cook are very generous. They give us food whenever we beg for it — crackers, cookies, candy and treats — in addition to our daily ration."

"Do you know that the collie at the Smith's house is going to have puppies?" asked Jenny. Shadow was not interested in such gossip at all, but Jenny knew all the local gossip. She knew about every dog marriage that was taking place in the neighborhood; she knew which dogs were expecting puppies; and which male and female dogs were going together.

"I have seen the Jones' terrier and the Brown's terrier together a great deal lately. I think we can expect a wedding announcement very soon," said Jenny. Shadow ignored that remark, but then she said instead: "Look at those beautiful clouds. If you look carefully you can actually see shapes like dogs. There is a spaniel, and there is the face of a bulldog, and there way over to the right are a few puppies. You can even see people," said Shadow.

The clouds didn't interest Jenny at all. Nor did any of the other things that Shadow always talked about — things like rocks, flowers, trees, the sunrise and sunset, even the falling rain.

If Shadow wasn't busy talking, she was thinking about something, and Jenny just couldn't stand thinking dogs. But deep in her heart she was very fond of

Shadow and knew that Shadow would stand up for her in time of trouble.

"Let's go for a walk," said Jenny. "Sure, why not?" said Shadow.

Jenny was surprised at Shadow's answer because she was used to the fact that Shadow was a good dog who never did anything she wasn't supposed to do. Jenny was expecting an answer like, "Oh, no — you know we are not allowed to leave the garden on our own."

"I know a hole in the fence at the

other end of the yard, because if we go through the gate the cook might see us from the kitchen window," said Jenny.

They dashed through the hole down at the end of the garden and within seconds they were off the property and out on the main road.

"Let's walk down to the river," said Jenny. Reaching the river they sat down to catch their breath while they watched a few boats go by.

"Ever been on a boat?" asked Jenny.

"No, but I always wanted to," replied Shadow.

"Maybe if we sit here in plain sight somebody will stop and pick us up." But nobody paid any attention to the two dogs sitting on the bank of the river.

"Let's swim out and pretend that we are drowning, and then somebody is bound to pick us up in their boat," said Jenny.

"Never play with death," advised Shadow. But Jenny didn't hear her and dashed out into the water, swimming out toward the middle of the river.

"Maybe it's a good idea after all," thought Shadow, and quickly jumped into the water also.

There was a motor boat with two young men on their way to a party in a village further up the river. When they saw Jenny and Shadow swimming in the water, they slowed down to get a better look.

"Let's pick them up and bring them

to the party," said one of the boys. And this is exactly what the dogs had hoped would happen.

"Funny-looking dogs," said one.

"It's only because they are wet," said his friend. Meanwhile, Jenny and Shadow were greatly enjoying the ride — all the while briskly and repeatedly shaking themselves dry.

"Okay, Mr. Black, we are here," said one of the young men to Shadow. He's so stupid, thought Shadow, since he doesn't even know a female from a male dog when he sees one!

"And you, Mrs. Rag, come along with me," said the other fellow to Jenny. The dog felt insulted being called "Mrs. Rag," but she decided to forgive the man because he really had no way of knowing that she had such a beautiful name as Jenny.

A young man docked the boat, and the four of them walked up to a big and beautiful summer-house. And here were gathered a bunch of young writers, both men and women. It was going to be a somewhat upscale literary party.

Everybody stared when the two men walked up with the wet dogs. One of the men said: "I would like you to meet two very good friends of mine: Mrs. Rag, editor of the *Canine Evening News*; and Mr. Black, the successful publisher of *Playdog* magazine." Everybody heartily laughed and clapped their hands.

"They are making fun of us," said

Shadow to Jenny. "Would you like a drink, Mrs. Rag?" said another man. "Maybe a dry martini, so you can dry off quickly?" Everybody then laughed and clapped their hands again. The dogs felt even more humiliated, of course. They crawled away toward the wall of the garden and laid down.

In a little while the music started to play and people began to dance. One man walked over to Jenny and said:

"Mrs. Rag, may I have the pleasure

of this dance?" Again, everybody laughed.

"Listen," said Shadow to Jenny, "next time the door opens, be ready to run!"

It was getting dark, the lights were turned down low, and almost everybody was dancing. The dogs laid very quiet. Then they heard footsteps outside.

"Be ready!" said Shadow. The door opened and in walked a couple. In a flash the dogs dashed through the door, and ran away as fast as they could.

"But how can we find our way home from here?" asked Jenny.

"Very simple," said Shadow, "we just run along the river."

"But in which direction?" asked Jenny as they reached the river.

"Do you see that big light all the way down on the other side of the river? That's Palisades Amusement Park, just opposite our house," said Shadow.

"Shadow, you are wonderful," said

Jenny.

"Wisdom comes with age," said Shadow playfully as they started on the journey home.

In the meantime, the maid and the cook were out looking all over the neighborhood for the dogs. The cook had been crying for an hour, "What a terrible thing! And what would the people say when they come back and find out that the dogs are lost?" She was just about to call the police when she heard something outside.

"They are back!" the cook cried out as the maid came running.

It is hard to say who was the happiest at that moment — was it Shadow, Jenny, the maid or the cook? It's also hard to say who was the most exhausted at the end of what turned out to be a very long and exciting day.

That night Jenny kept thinking how happy she was to be home again. "But at least," she thought to herself, "we finally got to ride in a boat!"

"Experience is what best makes us wise," Shadow thought to herself as she settled down to get some much-needed sleep.

## THE BIRTHDAY PARTY

In a big house in England, not far from London, lived a female dog named Sheba. She had been with this family, who was named Brown, for about three years. Back then Sheba had been brought to them by some friends who asked if they would like to own a dog. The previous owner, an old lady, had just died, but none of her relatives were really interested in adopting Sheba.

Mrs. Brown thought it was a shame to put such a beautiful dog to sleep, so she decided to keep her. A baby named Allan had just been born in the house, so she figured it would be good for him to get to know and grow up with a dog. Sheba would make a good babysitter, too.

Nobody knew exactly how old the dog was, but Sheba did. This coming Saturday she would be 7 years of age, and she decided that this year she would finally have a birthday party. That evening she went around to all the houses in the neighborhood, where she knew dogs lived. Almost every house had a dog, so she invited them for 4 o'clock Saturday afternoon in the Brown's garden. All of the dogs were very excited about the party; most of them could hardly wait.

For two whole weeks Sheba had been saving every bone and dog biscuit Mrs. Brown had given her. She carried the food down to the garden where the party was going to be held and hid everything safely in her doghouse.

One morning Allan, the boy, asked his mama: "Why doesn't Sheba eat her bone under the kitchen table anymore?"

"Well, I guess she wants to eat it outside in peace," said Mrs. Brown.

Allan seemed disappointed; he always liked to watch Sheba gnaw on a bone and crunch up her biscuits.

Saturday finally came and Sheba had everything prepared. She had dug little holes for seats, and beside each seat she put a bone and some biscuits. She had just enough, not counting herself. But she was willing to wait until supper, as long as it was enough for her guests. She felt a little bad; it was not much she had to offer them. But what could she do? She never liked to go out and steal food.

At exactly 4 o'clock the guests started to arrive. First came Falk, the German shepherd; then Blackie, the poodle; also Dyna, the Labrador with her three puppies; followed by Max the dachshund; then Jake, a mixed breed; and finally Nick, the miniature pinscher.

Everybody shook Sheba's paw, licked her face and wished her a happy birthday. She also got small gifts from everybody. There were a few crackers, three sticks, one bone, and little Nick kindly brought her one of his own toys, a rubber ball.

Sheba welcomed everybody and asked them to sit down and eat. It did not take long before all the food had disappeared, and Sheba then felt very embarrassed that she did not have anything more to offer her guests.

But she soon forgot her sad thoughts when one of the dogs stood up to deliver a speech. It was Jake and here is what he had to say:

"My dear Birthday Queen, dogs and puppies! I have something to say. When all of us from the neighborhood are happily gathered here on such a big day, we want you to know, darling Sheba, that you are not only a wonderful dog, but everyone's best friend in sunshine, rain, fog and snow!"

All the dogs clapped their paws and barked their approval, thinking it was a beautiful speech. Sheba was so touched she had to wipe away a few tears.

That afternoon, Allan was in the house playing with his toys. But after a while he got tired of playing and walked over to the window. He climbed up on a chair and started to look out over the garden. Then he discovered the dogs.

"Mommie, come and look at all the dogs!" he shouted excitedly. Mrs. Brown, who was doing some ironing in the kitchen, came over to the living-room window. Allan wanted to get some cookies and go down to feed the dogs. And when Mrs. Brown saw all those beautiful animals seated in a circle, she did not have the heart to say no. She gave Allan a full bag of her homemade cookies, and together they walked down to the garden.

Allan petted all the dogs and gave them the cookies. They were very happy, but the happiest dog of them all was Sheba, who now felt she was not such a bad hostess after all.

"Come, let us watch the dogs from the window," said Mrs. Brown, as she took Allan's hand. When they got to the house, the dogs were already starting to leave. The party was over. Only Sheba remained. She walked up towards the house. It had been a long day but she couldn't be happier. She ate a quick supper and went to bed. Shortly after, she was asleep. But as she slept, she was wagging her tail and dreaming about the wonderful birthday party.

Made in the USA
Charleston, SC
15 April 2015